No More Teasing!

Emma Chichester Clark

A

Andersen Press
London

for Milly and O

Other books by Emma Chichester Clark:

Happy Birthday to You, Blue Kangaroo!

I Love You, Blue Kangaroo!

Amazing Mr Zooty!

Will and Squill

Eliza and the Moonchild

Copyright © 2004 by Emma Chichester Clark
This paperback edition first published in 2005 by Andersen Press Ltd.
The rights of Emma Chichester Clark to be identified as the author and illustrator
of this work have been asserted by her in accordance with the Copyright, Designs and Patents Act, 1988.
First published in Great Britain in 2004 by Andersen Press Ltd., 20 Vauxhall Bridge Road, London SW1V 2SA.
Published in Australia by Random House Australia Pty., 20 Alfred Street, Milsons Point, Sydney, NSW 2061.
All rights reserved. Colour separated in Switzerland by Photolitho AG, Zürich.
Printed and bound in Italy by Grafiche AZ, Verona.

10   9   8   7   6   5   4   3   2

British Library Cataloguing in Publication Data available.

ISBN 978 1 84270 470 7

This book has been printed on acid-free paper

My cousin, Momo, is bigger than me.
I really like him, but he teases me,
all day long.

He says I'm a copycat.
But I'm not.

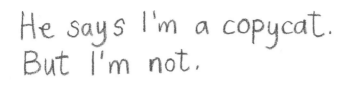

He calls me
names like
Titchypoo
and
Wee wee pants.

Titchypoo!

He says I am
SO stupid.
But I'm not.
He says the Grizzly Grilla will get me...

One day, he said I could play in his tree-house.
I thought that was really nice of him, but...

... he took the ladder away. He said the Grizzly Grilla was coming to get me. He said I was a scaredy pants. But I'm not!

scaredy pants!

Another time, he took my bear. He said he was
going to feed it to the Grizzly Grilla. He said
I was a crybaby. But I'm not . . .

Momo said if I walked the plank, I could have my bear back.

But he jumped up and down on it, and it was hard to stay on...

...so I fell in.

He said the Grizzly Grilla was coming.

He said I was a baby.
But I'm not.
I'm really not!

"I'm going!" I said. "And I'm never coming back!"

"Teeny wee wee baby Mimi!" said Momo.

"I'll show you, Big poo!" I said.

"The Grizzly Grilla will get you!"
he shouted.

I marched away, through the tall trees.
"I WON'T LET him tease me again," I said.

I marched on and on, and then, suddenly . . .

...what was that?

It must be the Grizzly Grilla!

I started to run···

...I ran,
as fast as
I could...
...and then,

BUMP!

I ran straight into Grandma!

She was collecting wood for the fire.
"Grandma! I thought you were the Grizzly
Grilla!" I said.

"Grizzly Grilla?"
said Grandma. "There's no
such thing! Who's been
teasing you?"
So I told her.

"Well, I think it's
time we did some
teasing of our own!"
said Grandma.
"Let me tell you
my plan..."

I found Momo playing on his drums.
"Run!" I shouted. "Run for your life! The Grizzly Grilla is coming!"

"Don't be such a baby," said Momo. "There's no such thing."

"He's coming," I cried, "he really REALLY is!"
"Grow up!" said Momo.
"I'm coming! I'm coming, and I'm looking for YOU!"
growled a deep gruff voice.

"Don't eat me!" cried Momo.

He was really scared.

Then,
the Grilla
gave me a
special
sign.

"STOP!" I shouted.
"NO MORE TEASING!"
The Grilla stopped.
"No more teasing!"
I said again.

"What did she say?"
roared the Grilla.
"No more teasing,"
whispered Momo.

"NO MORE TEASING!" growled the Grilla, in its deep dark voice. It took my hand and we walked away.

"I don't think Momo will tease you anymore," said Grandma.

"He might," I said, "but I know what I'll do."

"What will you do?" asked Grandma.

"I'll just laugh and laugh," I said,
"and then I'll growl a great big Grilla growl,
and I'll say NO MORE TEASING!"
"I think that will work," said Grandma, "don't you, Momo?"
"Mmm..." said Momo. "I think it might!"